D1361589

1

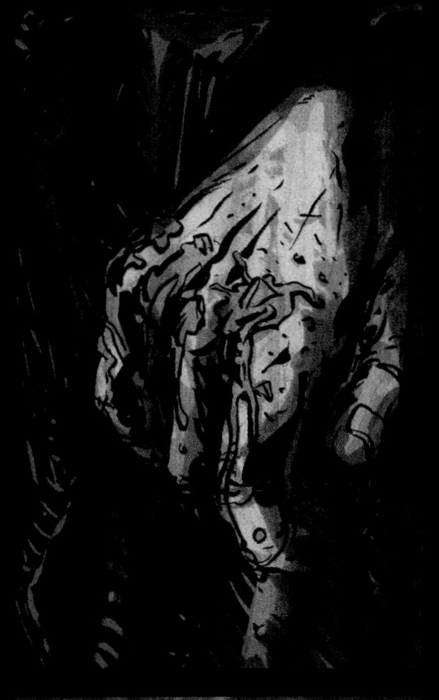

ALEX.

ALEX.

ALEX.

HHHUUGHHH.
WHERE-- WHAT IS THIS? WHERE AM I?
ALEX, WE DON'T HAVE MUCH TIME.
SO YOU NEED TO LISTEN TO ME CLOSELY.
YOU'RE OUR ONLY HOPE FOR ENDING THIS.
NO...NO NO. YOU'RE *DEAD*, WATKINS. I SAW YOU DIE.

THEY'RE COMING FOR YOU, ALEX, BUT YOU CANNOT, UNDER ANY CIRCUMSTANCE, LET THEM CATCH YOU.
WE DON'T HAVE TIME FOR THIS, NOW--

THEN MAKE TIME. YOU'RE DEAD. I'M DEAD.
THIS IS EITHER SOME FUCKED-UP VERSION OF HEAVEN, OR SOMETHING ELSE IS GOING ON--AND I GET THE FEELING YOU KNOW WHAT IT IS.
LET'S START WITH THE BODY ON THE FLOOR--THIS YOUR HANDIWORK?
NO, ALEX...
OH GOD. GRACIE.
...IT'S YOURS.
WHAT GAME ARE YOU PLAYING, WATKINS? WHAT IS THIS?!
IT'S THEM--THEY'RE SETTING YOU UP SO MORE PEOPLE COME AFTER YOU, AND TO STUDY HOW YOU REACT. IT'S HOW THEY LEARN, HOW THEY BECOME MORE--
WHO'S "THEY?!"
SKKKKREEEEE
THAT IS THEM.

YOU HAVE TO FIND THE BLACK TOWER, BUT YOU CAN ONLY SEE IT IF YOUR MIND LETS YOU SEE IT. FIND IT, ALEX. AND DESTROY IT.
WHAT IS THIS PLACE, WATKINS? WHERE ARE WE?
FROM WHAT I CAN TELL...
...IT'S MEANT TO BE EARTH, OR SOMETHING LIKE IT. BUT, BELIEVE ME, WE ARE NOT ON OUR HOME PLANET.
NOW GO, I'LL COME FIND YOU WHEN I CAN.
SKKKKREEEEE
OKAY, OKAY. HERE WE GO.

NNNNGGGHHHH
THUMP
THUMP
THUMP
OUT THE WINDOW! HE WENT UP TO THE ROOF--GO, GET HIM!
I TAKE IT YOU DIDN'T SECURE THE PACKAGE?
HE WOKE UP, HE...I DON'T KNOW HOW, BUT HE CAME TO AND WAS ON ME. BUSTED MY FACE OPEN AND TOOK OFF.
YOU'RE FORGIVEN, BUT ONLY BECAUSE I SEE THE INEVITABILITY BEFORE ME.
NO AMOUNT OF FAILURE WILL DETER ME FROM MY GOAL.
I WILL HAVE ALEX FORD. HIS SOUL WILL BE MINE.

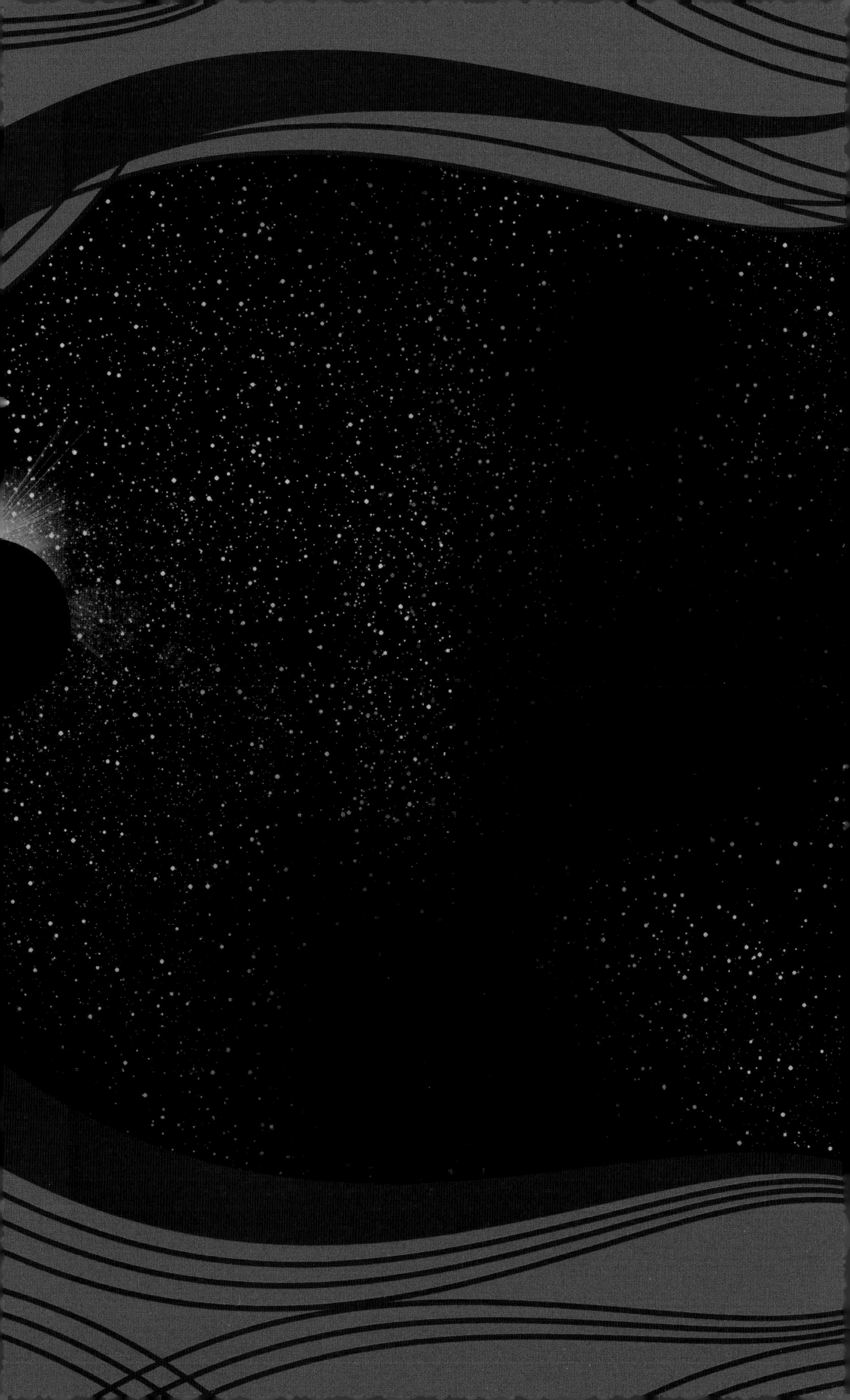

MAN SAYS IT'S DANGEROUS FOR YOU TO BE HERE SO MUCH. HE SAYS YOU'RE SPENDING TOO MUCH TIME LOOKING TO THE STARS.
IS THAT SO? AND WHAT DO *YOU* THINK?
I DON'T KNOW. I JUST WISH THE TELESCOPE WAS STRONG ENOUGH TO SEE YOUR ANUS.
IT'S YOUR-A-NIS. I'VE PROBABLY TOLD YOU THAT A HUNDRED TIMES.
I KNOW, BUT I LIKE TO MESS WITH YOU.
SO WHAT DO YOU DO IN THERE, SASHA? WHAT ARE YOU LOOKING FOR?
ARE YOU ASKING, GIRL, OR IS THIS MAN ASKING?
ME, I PROMISE. AND I WON'T TELL.
COME ON, I'LL SHOW YOU.

CCCCRRREEEEEE

WOOOOOOW. I CAN SEE WHY YOU'RE SUCH A HERMIT.
HEY!
WHAT? I MEANT IT IN A NICE WAY. I WOULDN'T GO OUTSIDE IF I HAD ALL THIS COOL STUFF EITHER.

COME HERE THEN--I WANT TO SHOW YOU THE COOLEST THING I'VE FOUND SO FAR.

SO, THE INTERESTING THING ABOUT THIS OBSERVATORY IS THAT IT ALSO HAS A RECEIVER, MEANING IT CAN PICK UP ALL SORTS OF NOISES FROM SPACE.
NOW I WANT YOU TO JUST BE QUIET AND LISTEN, THEN TELL ME WHAT YOU HEAR.

IT SOUNDS... HMMM. IT SOUNDS LIKE A RECORDING, LIKE VOICES. BUT THERE'S TOO MUCH STATIC, I CAN'T REALLY MAKE ANYT--
AHEM--

I THOUGHT I ASKED YOU TO NOT GO IN THE OBSERVATORY, YOUNG LADY.
NO, YOU SAID NOT TO GO POKING AROUND, BUT I WASN'T POKING AROUND. SASHA INVITED ME IN.
STILL, WE SHOULD GET BACK HOME. IT'S ALMOST DINNERTIME.
SASHA, CARE TO JOIN US?
YEAH SASHA, COME OVER FOR DINNER!
WELL, I'D LIKE TO BUT...
IT'S ALL RIGHT, MAYBE ONE DAY YOU'LL TAKE ME UP ON MY OFFER. OR, BETTER YET, MAYBE WE CAN GET YOU OUT ON THE BOAT FOR A RIDE ON THE LAKE.
NO, I'M SORRY, BUT I DEFINITELY WON'T BE DOING THAT.
SASHA, I'VE BEEN ON THAT LAKE, ALL OVER IT, DOZENS OF TIMES. THERE'S *NOTHING* OUT THERE.
I DON'T AGREE--I CAN'T GET PAST THIS FEELING THAT THERE *IS* SOMETHING OUT THERE...
"...SOMETHING TERRIBLE, AND I DON'T WANT TO FIND OUT WHAT."

"WELL...AT LEAST WE HAVE AN I.D. THIS TIME."
YOU KNOW THIS ONE, SONYA?
NAME'S GRACIE LYONS. SHE RUNS AN UNDERGROUND HIGH-END BROTHEL.
SHE'S WELL CONNECTED, VERY POWERFUL...
...WHICH BEGS THE QUESTION--HOW'D SHE END UP IN THIS DINGY FLOPHOUSE IN THE FIRST PLACE?
HEY, HEY! I GOT RIGHTS, MAN!
JUST GET IN THERE AND TELL HER WHAT YOU TOLD ME.
YEAH, AND WHAT'S IN IT FOR ME, HUH? WHAT'S THE REWARD HERE?
I ALREADY PAID YOU. NOW, IF YOU'D LIKE ME TO UN-PAY YOU AND COLLECT MY INTEREST IMMEDIATELY, THAT CAN BE ARRANGED.
ALL RIGHT, PIT BULL. CALM DOWN. WHO AM I TALKING TO?

PROPRIETOR OF THIS ESTABLISHMENT?
WON IT IN A CARD GAME. JUST IRONING OUT THE OFFICIAL PAPERWORK, OTHERWISE I'D HAVE IT FO--
WHO OWNS THIS DUMP. WHAT HAVE YOU GOT FOR ME?

I GOT RECALL KINGPIN ALEX FORD, THAT'S WHAT I GOT.
ENTERING THIS BUILDING EARLIER TONIGHT WITH THE DECEASED HERSELF.

SON OF A *BITCH*.

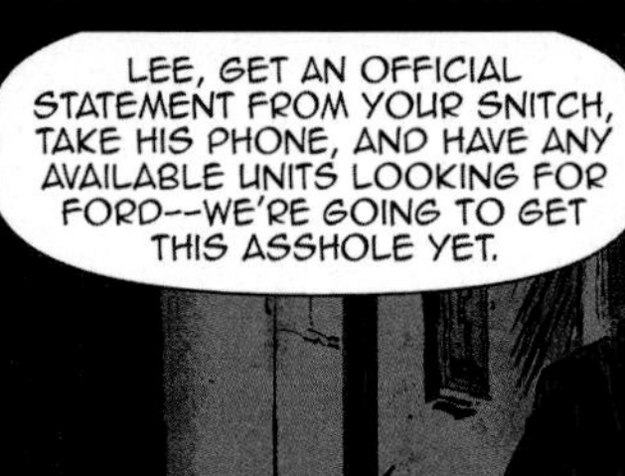
LEE, GET AN OFFICIAL STATEMENT FROM YOUR SNITCH, TAKE HIS PHONE, AND HAVE ANY AVAILABLE UNITS LOOKING FOR FORD--WE'RE GOING TO GET THIS ASSHOLE YET.

OKAY, SURE. AND WHERE THE HELL ARE YOU GOING?

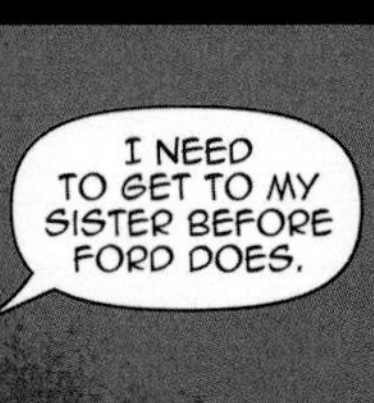
I NEED TO GET TO MY SISTER BEFORE FORD DOES.

"HELLO? HELLO THERE?"
"HEY, YOU, UP AND AT IT."
YEAH, WHAT? WHAT IS IT?
DOES THIS TRAIN GO TO THE BLACK TOWER?
JUST HEAD DOWN THOSE STAIRS OVER THERE AND HOP ON THE NEXT TRAIN...
"...IT'S THE ONLY ONE RUNNING AT THIS TIME OF NIGHT."
EXCUSE ME, SIR?

I'M LOOKING FOR THE TRAIN THAT'LL TAKE ME OUT TO THE BLACK TOWER. DO YOU KNOW WHICH ONE WILL GET ME THERE?
THE BLACK TOWER? NEVER KNOWN ANYONE WANTING TO GO OUT THERE-- SOMETIMES THINK IT'S A MYTH MYSELF. I THINK YOU WANT THE SOUTH TRACK, 'CROSS STATION.
WHAT THE HELL?
THE GRAY LINE. HURRY AND YOU CAN CATCH THE NEXT ONE COMING IN JUST A FEW MINUTES.
THIS IS THE LAST STOP FOR THIS LINE. ALL PASSENGERS MUST GET OFF THIS TRAIN.
DOESN'T THIS TRAIN GO TO THE BLACK TOWER?
NOPE, GOES RIGHT HERE. COULDN'T TELL YOU WHICH TRAIN STILL RUNS OUT THAT WAY.
ALEX, ALEX--YOU'RE GOING TO

...YOU WOULDN'T WANT TO GIVE PEOPLE THE IMPRESSION THAT YOU'RE TRYING TO RUN OFF.
WOODBURY. YOU WOULDN'T KNOW HOW TO GET TO THE BLACK TOWER, WOULD YOU?
SURE. WHY DON'T YOU HOP IN MY CAR--I'LL TAKE YOU DIRECTLY THERE.
SMARTS AND MUSCLE-- THAT'S WHY GRACIE ALWAYS LIKED YOU.
SPEAKING OF. WHAT THE FUCK DID YOU DO TO HER? AND WHY?
I KNOW THIS DOESN'T LOOK GOOD, WOODBURY, BUT I DON'T KNOW WHAT HAPPENED TO GRACIE. THERE'S SOMETHING GOING ON, SOMETHING VERY STRANGE, AND I JUST NEED SOME TIME TO--
ENOUGH. LADIES, TAKE THIS ASSHOLE.

WHY DID YOU KILL HER?!
I DON'T EVEN REMEMBER BEING WITH HER, BUT I WOKE UP AND--
OOOFF
RUNNING OUT OF REAL ESTATE, FORD. JUST COME CLEAN, AND WE'LL GO EASY ON YOU.
YOU'LL HAVE TO FORGIVE
KAFF KAFF
MY LACK OF ENTHUSIASM...
...FOR AN ANGRY MOB'S IDEA OF "EASY."

ALEX.
I CAN STILL SEE YOU, IDIOT.
CCRRKK
LET ME TELL YOU WHAT AN IDIOT DOES, WOODBURY.

AN IDIOT WOULD HOT WIRE THIS TRAIN WITHOUT HAVING A WAY TO MAKE IT STOP.
ANYBODY ON BOARD WILL JUST HAVE TO TAKE THEIR CHANCES.

LET'S GO, OFF, OFF!
I DIDN'T DO A THING TO GRACIE, I WANT YOU ALL TO KNOW THAT. SOMEONE SET ME UP, AND I'M GOING TO FIND OUT WHO THAT PERSON IS.
AND WOODBURY, THERE IS A WAY TO SLOW THIS THING DOWN...
IT'S CALLED THE BRAKES. WHO'S THE IDIOT NOW?
LET'S TURN OVER SOME MORE STONES. IN CASE FORD IS TELLING THE TRUTH AND SOMEONE ELSE IS RESPONSIBLE, THEY ARE NOT GOING TO GET AWAY WITH IT.

HOLD THAT ELEVATOR.
THANKS.
YEAH...
...NO PROBLEM.

OOOFF
AAGGGHHH

DING

MMMPPPFFF
I'M SORRY...I'M SORRY.
BUT ALEX HAS A JOB TO DO.
CHRIST, SHE DAMN NEAR BROKE BY SKULL IN HALF.
WALK IT OFF. WE NEED TO GET HER TO THE LAB.
I GET THE FEELING SHE'S GOING TO NEED TO SEE WHAT'S GOING ON TO BELIEVE IT.

"IT'S A BEAUTIFUL SKY, ISN'T IT?"
HAS A WAY OF MESMERIZING YOU?
IT DOES, YES...BUT, ARE YOU LOOKING FOR SOMEONE?

DON'T MIND ME, I'M JUST AN OLD SOUL AND STARGAZER LIKE YOURSELF, LOOKING OUT TO THE NIGHT SKY AND WONDERING WHERE ALL THAT DISTANCE CAN TAKE US. YOU BEEN WATCHING THIS PATCH OF SKY FOR A LONG TIME?
I...I THINK SO, YEAH. I CAN'T REALLY REMEMBER HOW LONG I'VE BEEN HERE. NOT SOMETHING I REALLY THINK ABOUT.
STRANGE, WOULDN'T YOU SAY?

WELL, I KNOW I'VE BEEN AROUND LONG ENOUGH TO KNOW THAT THERE'RE MORE STARS IN THE SKY ALL THE TIME.
I CAN'T EVEN KEEP TRACK OF THEM ALL ANYMORE.
OH, SASHA...

THOSE AREN'T STARS.

UMMM, I'M SORRY. HAVE WE MET BEFORE?
YES AND NO. BUT, AS YOU ALLUDED TO YOURSELF, THE PAST ISN'T SOMETHING WE CAN ACCOUNT FOR IN THIS PLACE.
WHAT MATTERS IS THE MOMENTS WE'RE IN, AND HOW WE CHOOSE TO DEFINE THEM.
NOW, MORE THAN EVER, YOU HAVE TO MOLD YOUR WORLD.
LOOK, IT'S GETTING LATE, AND I SHOULD GET INSIDE. IT WAS NICE TALKING TO Y--
THE TRANSMISSION YOU'VE BEEN RECEIVING-- RECALIBRATE THE SATELLITE'S POSITION BY 17 METERS NORTHEAST.
AND WHAT? WHAT WILL I HEAR?
WHAT YOU NEED TO.

CRAZY OLD MAN.
"WHAT YOU NEED TO." THE HELL DOES THAT MEAN, ANYWAY?
GOD DAMN IT.
SATELLITE POSITIONING CALIBRATION
...KEEP THIS TRANSMISSION GOING AS LONG AS WE'RE ABLE TO
IF YOU'RE LISTENING, KNOW THIS IS NOT A HOAX. WE HAVE FOUND A WAY TO *END* THIS.
AGAIN, THIS IS LIEUTENANT--
HOLY SHIT...

ELBUS.

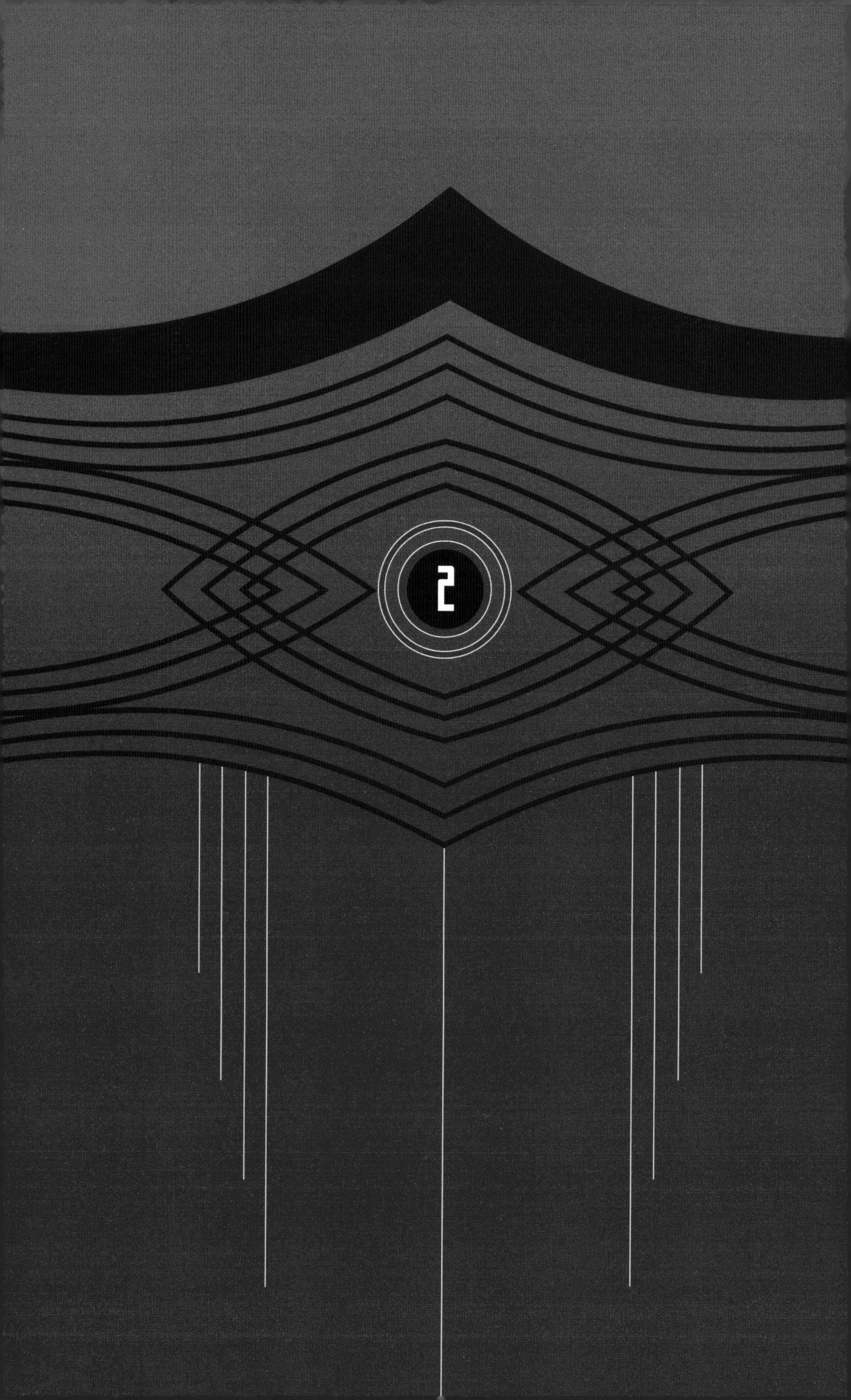
2

"JESUS CHRIST."
YOU'VE GOT TO BE FUCKING KIDDING ME.
OF COURSE THERE'S A BRICK WALL CUTTING OFF THE ONLY TRAIN THAT GOES TO THIS ALLEGED TOWER.
OF COURSE.
"YOU CAN ONLY REVEAL IT WITH YOUR MIND," JEDI MASTER WATKINS SAYS.
YEAH, SURE THING.

REVEAL IT WITH YOUR MIND, REVEAL IT WITH YOUR MIND...
CAVE

ALL RIGHT...ALL RIGHT.
SHADOW
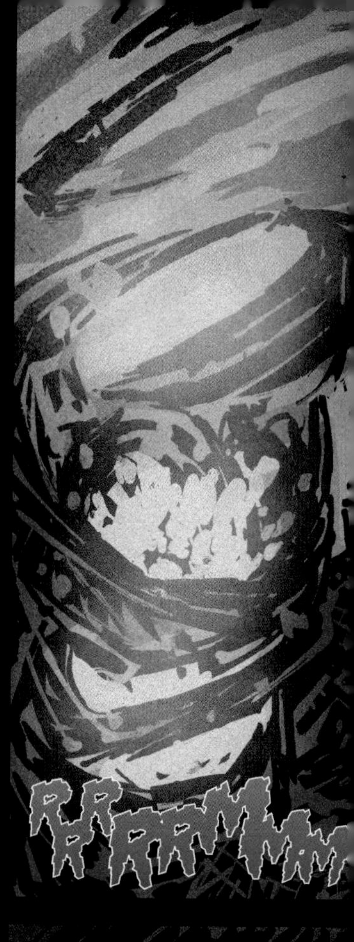
RRRRRRMMMM

RRRRRRMMMM

OH MY GOD.

THE BLACK TOWER.

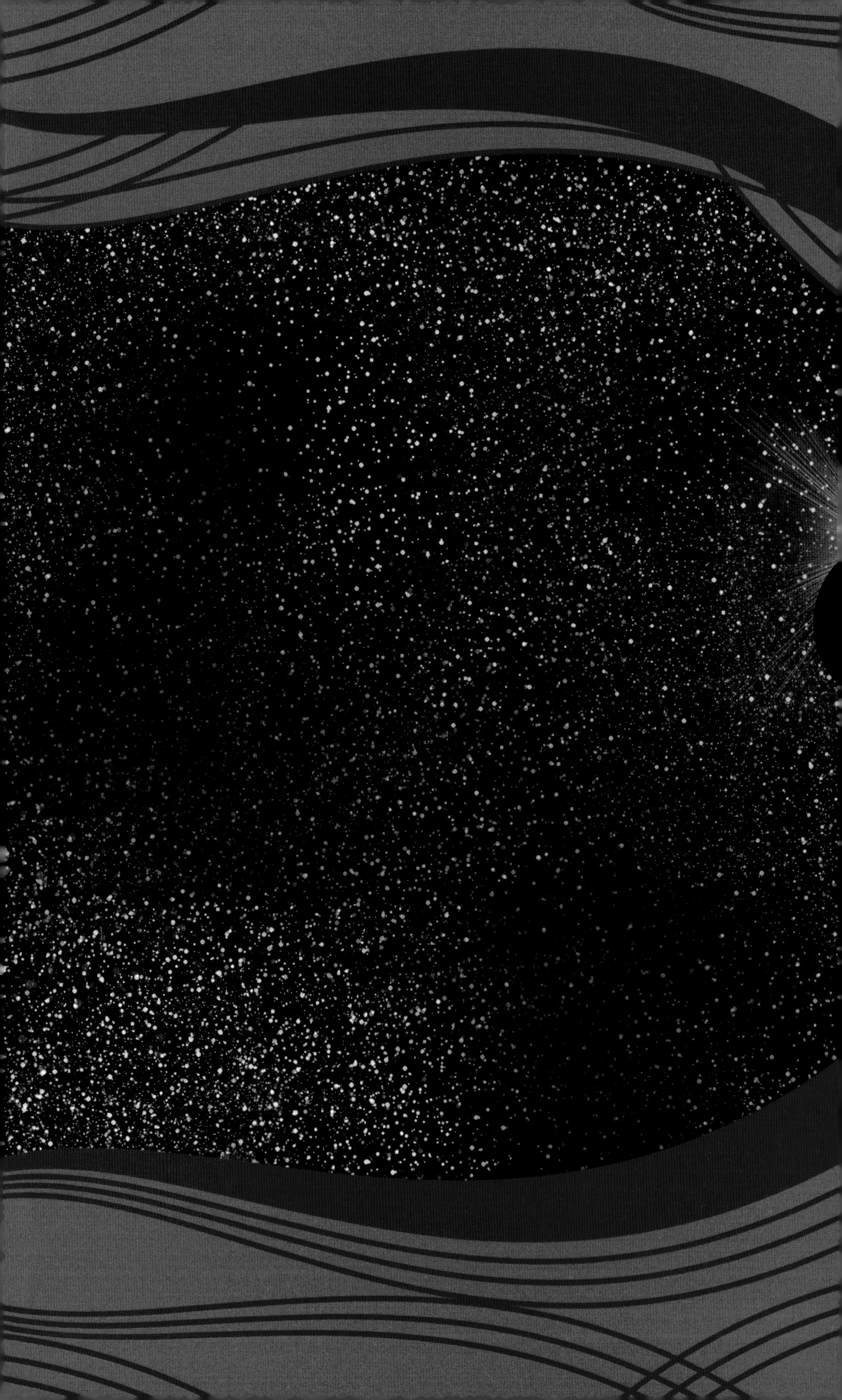

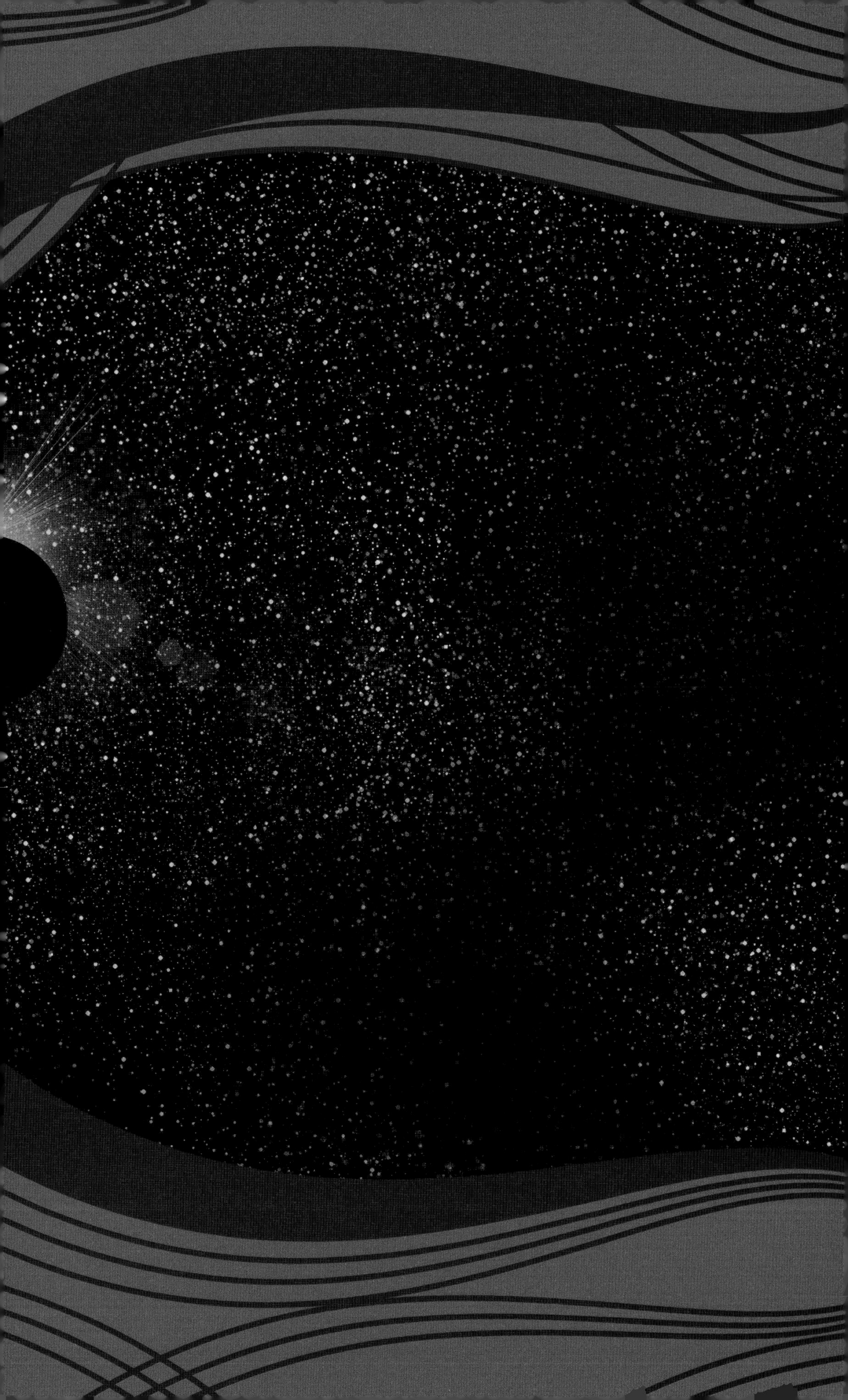

SASHA! HEY, SASHA!
GO BACK HOME, SWEETIE. FIND YOUR DAD AND STAY WITH HIM-- DO **NOT** LEAVE HIS SIDE.

WHAT DO YOU MEAN? AND I THOUGHT YOU WERE AFRAID OF THE WATER. YOU SAID A **MONSTER** LIVES IN IT.
I STILL THINK THAT MIGHT ACTUALLY BE THE CASE. BUT I HAVE TO GO-- THERE'S SOMETHING I **HAVE** TO DO.

LISTEN, THERE IS... **SO MUCH** I NEED TO TELL YOU. BUT I NEED TO FIGURE OUT WHAT'S HAPPENING TO ME--TO ALL OF US--FIRST. AND WHILE I DO THAT, I NEED TO BE SURE YOU'RE SAFE.
PROMISE ME YOU'LL STAY WITH YOUR DAD AND **DON'T** WANDER OFF UNTIL I GET BACK.
BUT WHEN WILL YOU BE BACK? I'M AFRAID TO SEE YOU GO.
YEAH...

...THAT MAKES TWO OF US.

SASHA, I REALLY DON'T THINK YOU SHOULD BE DOING THIS--IT DOESN'T SEEM *RIGHT*.
WELL, I THINK WHATEVER PUT US HERE--WHEREVER *HERE* IS--HAS MADE IT SO YOU THINK THAT WAY. YOU SEEM TO BE PROGRAMMED TO KEEP ME HERE.

SASHA, WAIT.

SOMETHING ABOUT YOU LEAVING... IT MAKES ME SCARED IN A WAY I DON'T THINK I'VE EVER FELT BEFORE. SASHA, PLEASE...I CAN'T EXPLAIN WHY, BUT I REALLY DON'T WANT YOU TO GO.

THERE'S A REASON YOU FEEL THAT WAY, AND IT'S BECAUSE OF ME. IT'S BECAUSE...

...BECAUSE I'VE DONE IT TO YOU BEFORE.

I DON'T UNDERSTAND, SASHA.
NO, AND YOU SHOULDN'T. AND I'M NOT SURE THERE'S ANY WAY FOR ME TO EXPLAIN EVERYTHING I KNOW IN A WAY THAT MAKES SENSE.

I HAVE AN IDEA, THOUGH. BECAUSE...I CAN'T. I CAN'T LEAVE YOU BOTH AGAIN.

GLIDING O'ER ALL, THROUGH ALL,THROUGH NATURE, TIME, AND SPACE,THE VOYAGE OF THE SOUL-- NOT LIFE ALONE, DEATH, MANY DEATHS I'LL SING.

SASHA?

WHAT... WHERE ARE WE? *WHAT IS THIS?*
I DON'T KNOW, I REALLY DON'T. BUT WE HAVE TO GO. THERE'S SOMETHING I NEED, AND WE'RE NOT GOING TO FIND IT HERE.
UMMM...DOES ANYONE WANT TO TELL ME WHY YOU TWO ARE SUDDENLY MAKING OUT? ALSO-- GROSS.
WELL... WHERE ARE WE EVEN GOING? AND ARE YOU SURE THIS RICKETY BOAT WILL GET US THERE?
STAYING HERE IS NOT AN OPTION, THAT'S THE ONE THING I'M CERTAIN OF.

AND, SWEETIE, I'LL FIND A WAY TO GET YOU TO UNDERSTAND ALL THIS. I PROMISE.
YEAH, I'M WITH YOU ON THAT.
THIS IS ALL REALLY WEIRD.

WHEREVER WE ARE RIGHT NOW, IT'S ALL I KNOW OF THIS PLACE. I CAN'T EVEN IMAGINE WHAT'S OUT THERE, WHAT'S BEYOND THE WATER.
WHATEVER IT IS, DAVE, I SUGGEST WE BRING A GUN. IN MY EXPERIENCE, WE MAY NEED IT.

KKKREEEEE
SHIT.
HEY, ASSHOLE...
...I DON'T KNOW IF YOU'RE THE WORST BURGLAR EVER OR IF YOU'RE ATTEMPTING SUICIDE BY STUPIDITY. AND I REALLY DON'T CARE. I WANT YOU OUT OF HERE NOW, OR I'LL BLOW OUT YOUR KNEECAPS.
WHOA WHOA WHOA.
IT'S ME, BEKKAH. IT'S JUST ME.

JESUS, ALEX. WHAT THE HELL ARE YOU DOING BREAKING INTO MY APARTMENT?
BEING SAFE--THEY MIGHT HAVE EYES ON YOUR PLACE.
THEY? AND...HUH?
BEKKAH, I NEED YOU TO TRUST ME ON THIS-- BUT WE NEED TO GET OUT OF HERE. WE NEED TO GET AS FAR AWAY AS POSSIBLE, AND WE NEED TO DO IT NOW.
ALL OF THIS, EVERYTHING AROUND US-- NOTHING IS WHAT WE THINK IT IS.
COME ON, WE CAN SNEAK OUT THROUGH THE BASEMENT AND--
WAIT, JUST WAIT. ALEX, FIRST OF ALL, WE CAN'T GO ANYWHERE ELSE. EVERYTHING BEYOND THE CITY IS DEAD. THE WORLD WAS OBLITERATED, WE BOTH KNOW THAT.
YEAH, MAYBE-- ASSUMING WE'RE ON EARTH, WHICH I DON'T THINK WE ARE.
IT'S CRAZY, I KNOW. BUT SOMETHING'S HAPPENING, SOMETHING BAD. AND I SWEAR--I SWEAR--I'LL EXPLAIN EVERYTHING TO YOU ONCE WE'RE SAFE.
BUT FOR RIGHT NOW, WE HAVE TO--

HELLO, ALEX.
HOLY SHIT-- NO.
5G
YOU WILL NOT ESCAPE. WE NEEDED YOU TO HELP COMPLETE OUR MISSION. NEEDED TO STUDY YOU, UNDERSTAND YOU.
BUT WE'VE NEARLY UNLOCKED YOUR HUMAN CODE, AND THAT MAKES YOU... SUPERFLUOUS.
AND A DANGEROUS ONE AT THAT.

WHAT... WHAT ARE THESE THINGS?
BEKKAH.... HOLD ON TO ME. *TIGHT*.

ALEX? *ALEX?!* WHAT ARE YOU--

JUST HOLD ON!

KKKKSSSSHHHH
AAAAHHHHH!

OOOFFF

SNAP
BEKKAH, TURN! TURN AWAY FROM THE BUIL--

OOOFFF
ALEX... ARE YOU ALL RIGHT?
I'M -KAFF KAFF- I'M FINE. COME ON, WE HAVE TO... NNNGGGHH...KEEP MOVING.
FIRE
SHADOWS ON THE WALL
ALEX!
AAAAHHH

YOU CAN'T DO THAT TO SOMEONE-- HE CAN BE HURT!
WE HAVE TO GO. BESIDES, HE'S NOT REAL.
NONE OF THIS IS REAL.

VVVRRRRRRMMMM
MY PETS...
...PURSUE.

HHHYYKKK
GOOD, YOU'RE AWAKE AT LAST. COME ON, I'D LIKE TO SHOW YOU SOMETHING.
WHAT-- WHAT IS THIS PLACE? WHERE AM I?
YOU'RE IN MY LAB, AND I'D LIKE YOU TO NOTICE YOU HAVEN'T BEEN BOUND OR RESTRAINED. YOU'RE NO PRISONER.
YOU SON OF A--
WHOA THERE.. YOU'RE GONNA WANT TO TAKE IT EASY FOR A FEW MINUTES.
YOU DRUGGED ME-- WHAT DID YOU DO TO ME? WHY AM I *HERE*?
I APOLOGIZE FOR THAT--I COULDN'T THINK OF ANY OTHER WAY OF GETTING YOU HERE.
ALLOW ME TO SHOW YOU ONE THING, JUST ONE. IF YOU'RE UNMOVED, YOU CAN ARREST ME--BOTH OF US. WE'LL GO WILLINGLY.
THIS WAY.

IF I CAN ASK ONE MORE THING-- KEEP AN OPEN MIND.
I'M FOLLOWING A MAN WHO DRUGGED AND ABDUCTED ME TO A SECRET LAIR. DON'T PUSH IT.
REMEMBER, SONYA. THINK BACK, THINK HARD.
REMEMBER.
WHY-- WHY DO YOU HAVE THESE?
UNFORTUNATELY, SONYA...
OH MY GOD.

...I'VE BEEN PERFORMING EXPERIMENTS FOR THE ENEMY. THE ALIENS FROM THE ANOMALY--THEY BROUGHT ME HERE, BROUGHT ALL OF US HERE, FOR SPECIFIC REASONS.
MINE HAS BEEN TO HELP THEM CAPTURE THE ESSENCE OF HUMANITY. WE ARE UNIQUE IN WAYS WE FAIL TO APPRECIATE, SONYA. THE SAME THINGS WE'RE OFTEN BURDENED BY--SELF-AWARENESS, A CONSCIENCE, A FEELING OF SPIRITUALITY--ARE WHAT ALSO MAKE US UNLIKE ANYTHING ELSE IN THE UNIVERSE. AND THESE ALIENS WANT THAT FOR THEMSELVES.
THEY'RE CLOSE TO GETTING THERE. AND WHEN THEY DO, THEY'LL TAKE OVER THE EARTH--THE REAL EARTH.
THINK ABOUT IT. YOU KNOW YOU HAVE A PAST LIFE, A REAL LIFE.
THIS ISN'T IT.
EVEN IF I DID BELIEVE YOU--WHAT CAN I DO ABOUT ANY OF THIS?
HELP ALEX--THE ALIENS FAIL TO COMPREHEND HIS SOUL. SACRIFICE IS COUNTER TO THEIR IDEA OF THE INDIVIDUAL. NOW, THEY WENT HIM DEAD--THEY WANT HIM PURGED.
THAT STILL DOESN'T ANSWER MY QUESTION. WHAT CAN I DO, WHAT CAN ALEX OR ANY OF US DO TO STOP THESE THINGS?
THAT'S THE OTHER THING I NEED TO SHOW YOU.
WHAT THE FUCK?
I CALL IT THE BLACK TOWER. YOU CAN'T SEE UNLESS YOU'RE AWAKENED TO IT.
AT THE TOP IS THEIR KING, FEEDING ON THE HUMAN PLAY GOING ON ALL AROUND US. THE ALIENS ARE A HIVE, SO THE MOMENT HE LEARNS TO BE HUMAN--AND HE'S CLOSE--EARTH, AND EVERYONE ON IT, ARE DOOMED.
YOU HAVE TO FIND A WAY TO KILL HIM.

WHERE ARE WE GOING? AND WHAT THE HELL WERE THOSE THINGS?!
THEY'RE THINGS WE *REALLY* WANT TO AVOID. SO WE'RE GOING TO KEEP DRIVING UNTIL WE--
OH FUCK.
SKKKKKREEEEEE

NNGGHH
NO.
BLAM
BLAM
NO,
BEKK--

GUH!

ALEX?
IT'S POETIC, I SUPPOSE, THAT YOU HAVE BECOME OUR ANOMALY.
YOUR WILLINGNESS FOR SACRIFICE AND UNDERMINING YOUR MOST FUNDAMENTAL NEED AS AN INDIVIDUAL--TO SURVIVE--IS SOMETHING WE CAN'T PROCESS. NOR DO WE WANT TO.
YOUR SACRIFICE IS NOW TO US. TO BEING PURGED SO WE CAN BECOME A BETTER HUMAN THAN YOU COULD EVER BE. WE ABANDON YOUR WEAKNESS AND USHER IN A NEW--

SCCCRRRRCHHH
BLAM
BLAM
BLAM
BLAM
BEKKAH, LET'S GO!
BLAM
BLAM
BLAM
BLAM
BLAM
HAVE TO...GET... MOSCOW...
DON'T TALK, OKAY? JUST...JUST HOLD ON.
BLAM
BLAM
BLAM
BEKKAH...
WE NEED TO GET HIM TO A HOSPITAL. THERE HAS TO BE SOMETHING--

...WE NEED TO MAKE HIM COMFORTABLE.
NO.
YOU DID THIS! I'LL KILL... I'LL--
CLIK CLIK CLIK CLIK
BEKKAH, COME ON. THERE'S NOTHING ELSE WE CAN DO HERE EXCEPT GET TORN APART BY THESE THINGS.
WE HAVE TO GO.
"RUN. RUN TO NOWHERE."
"YOUR TIME IS OVER."

"SO, WHAT ABOUT THE TIME YOU LOST YOUR RETAINER ON THAT MEGA ROLLER COASTER. THAT RING A BELL?"
"NOPE."
"OKAY...THEN WHAT ABOUT WHEN WE WENT TO MOUNT RUSHMORE ON VACATION AND YOU MADE YOUR DAD PEE HIS PANTS A LITTLE LAUGHING ABOUT PICKING WASHINGTON'S ROCK NOSE?"
"HEY."

NOPE.
WELL, DON'T WORRY, OKAY? IT'LL COME TO YOU.
HEY, SASHA...

...THERE'S SOMETHING, THOUGH I DON'T KNOW *WHAT*, AHEAD.

WHAT IN THE HELL IS *THAT*?
NO...
...THAT'S *EXACTLY* WHERE WE'RE SUPPOSED TO BE.
MAYBE WE SHOULD TURN AROUND?

3

I KNOW... I KNOW NONE OF THIS IS REAL. BUT STILL...
I'M GOING TO MISS BEING ALIVE.
I HOPE YOUR LIFE WAS A HAPPY ONE. I HOPE YOU MADE A WORLD THAT WAS EVERY BIT AS BEAUTIFUL AS YOU DESERVE.
ALEX, I REMEMBER YOU-- I REMEMBER EVERYTHING. WHEN WE WERE BEING CHASED, IT ALL CAME BACK TO ME.
I WANT YOU TO KNOW THAT YOU WERE ALWAYS MY WORLD. WE'RE EACH OTHER'S, AND WE ALWAYS WILL BE.
I ONLY WISH...WISH WE HAD MORE TIME. WE COULD HAVE.. COULD HAV
ALEX?
ALEX.

UM... SONYA?
YOU'RE SEEING THIS, RIGHT?
I...YEAH, I AM. IS THAT...?
IT'S ALEX.

THIS GIVES ME AN IDEA.

"SHE MUST BE STARVING--THAT'S WHY SHE'S SLEEPING SO MUCH."

DO YOU REMEMBER THAT TIME SHE GOT SICK AT YOUR MOM'S CABIN? GOD, I'VE NEVER FELT SO *TRAPPED* IN MY ENTIRE LIFE. THE ROADS WERE TOO SLEEK WITH ICE, AND NO DOCTORS COULD SEE HER UNTIL MORNING ANYWAY.
SHE WAS THREE, AND SHE WAS JUST *SO* SICK. I DON'T EVEN LIKE THINKING ABOUT IT.

I HELD HER ALL NIGHT. JUST STAYED AWAKE AND HELD HER CLOSE. I HAD THIS FEAR, THIS *TERROR*, THAT IF I LOOSENED MY GRASP SHE'D BE GONE. SHE'D JUST... DISAPPEAR.

THIS IS ALL *MY FAULT*.

SASHA, NO-- YOU CAN'T SAY THAT. THAT'S NOT EVEN POSSIBLE.
WE'RE LIVING MY PSYCHE, DAVE. THE SMALL COTTAGE LIFE ON THE WATER, JUST THE THREE OF US, THAT WAS MY GREATEST DESIRE IN LIFE. THAT'S WHAT I ALWAYS WANTED FOR US.
AND THIS...

...MY GREATEST FEAR. PHYSICALLY LOSING OUR DAUGHTER. WATCHING HER DISAPPEAR BEFORE MY EYES.

I JUST...I WISH I KNEW WHY THIS IS HAPPENING. I WISH I KNEW WHERE WE ARE--WHERE WE REALLY ARE. IT HAS TO BE DISPATER, THAT GOD DAMN PLANET. AND, FOR WHATEVER REASON, WE WERE NOT SUPPOSED TO LEAVE THE COAST.
OKAY, OKAY... LET'S ASSUME YOU'RE RIGHT. THIS WORLD WE KNOW--MYSELF INCLUDED--IS ALL JUST AN EXTENSION OF YOU. YOUR MIND, YOUR SOUL. I'M NOT SURE I LOVE BEING A MANIFESTATION, BUT LET'S ROLL WITH IT.

IF YOU'RE CREATING THE ILLUSION, YOU CAN END IT AS WELL. WE ARE LOST IN THE MIDDLE OF NOWHERE, SASHA. ANCHOR US.
BUT IF I SEE THIS PLACE FOR WHAT IT REALLY IS, IF MY FANTASY ENDS, WHAT WILL HAPPEN TO YOU?

I DON'T THINK THAT WILL HAPPEN, MY LOVE. WE'RE WITH YOU EVERYWHERE YOU GO. ALWAYS.
NOW...

CLOSE YOUR EYES. FOCUS.

DON'T THINK OF ME, DON'T THINK OF ANY OF THESE ILLUSIONS. WHERE ARE YOU?
IT'S...IT'S *DARK*.

IT'S A CITY, LIKE THE COLONY THAT USED TO BE ON DISPATER. BUT...BUT IT'S NOT REAL EITHER. I THINK...I THINK IT'S THE WORLD ***THEY'VE*** CREATED.

THE BLACK SUN.
THEY MADE THIS WORLD, TRAPPED US HERE.

"AND THERE'S.... JESUS, THERE'S THIS TOWER. IT'S--DAVE?"

"DAVE?!"

MOM?

WE'RE HERE--WE'RE ALL HERE.
I REMEMBER, MOM. I REMEMBER YOU HOLDING ME, I REMEMBER FEELING BETTER BECAUSE YOU WERE HOLDING ME.

ANNIE. I'VE MISSED YOU--YOU HAVE NO IDEA.
SASHA, I'M GLAD YOU RESCUED US FROM THE NEVER-ENDING LAKE...

BUT WHERE ARE WE?

WE'RE EXACTLY WHERE WE NEED TO BE.
WE'RE GOING TO END THIS.

I--I'M SORRY. YOU WANT TO DO *WHAT*?
YOU CAN MANIPULATE SOULS, RIGHT? TAKE THEM OUT OF BODIES, SWAP THEM BETWEEN PEOPLE, MAKE NEW MEMORIES, ALL THAT CRAZY SHIT?
NOT BY CHOICE BUT, YES, THAT'S RIGHT.
OKAY, THEN WHAT WE WANT TO DO IS PRETTY STRAIGHT-FORWARD.
WE'RE GOING TO RIP MOSCOW'S SOUL FROM HIS BODY.
OKAY, THAT'S WHAT I THOUGHT YOU SAID. BUT...*WHY*? HOW? HE'S SURROUNDED BY THOSE ALIENS, AND YOU CAN ONLY FIND HIM AT THE BASE OF THE BLACK TOWER.
BUT YOU ARE CORRECT--SHOULD YOU MANAGE TO KILL HIM, HIS SOUL WILL EVACUATE. JUST LIKE YOU SAID ALEX'S DID.
THAT DOESN'T EXPLAIN HOW YOU CAN POSSIBLY PULL THIS OFF, THOUGH.
LEAVE THAT TO US.

I'M LIKING THE WHOLE URBAN HELLSCAPE VIBE THIS PLACE HAS GOING ON.
YEAH, I DON'T THINK THIS IS MEANT TO BE A FRIENDLY PLACE.
EVEN THOUGH EVERY QUESTION GIVES BIRTH TO THREE NEW ONES, I HAVE TO ASK: WHERE ARE WE GOING?
I'M NOT SURE. THE EQUIPMENT I HAD, IT ONLY RECEIVED INCOMING MESSAGES. I NEED SATELLITE COMMUNICATIONS THAT CAN *TRANSMIT*.
MY CREWMATES HAVE THAT MESSAGE PLAYING ON A LOOP, AND UNTIL I CAN GET IN TOUCH WITH THEM, I WON'T KNOW HOW I CAN HELP THEM.
AND, BELIEVE ME, IF ELBUS SAYS HE CAN WIPE THESE ALIENS OUT, THEY'RE AS GOOD AS DEAD. LANGFORD, THE GUY WHO MADE THE COLONY, HE HAD A COMPOUND HERE. I'D SAY WE TRY THERE FIR--

SKKKKREEEEEE
WHAT WAS THAT?
OH MY GOD.

RUN.

SKKKKREEEEE

MOM?!
GO, GO--KEEP GOING, DON'T LOOK BA--

SKKKKREEEEE

BLAM
BLAM
BLAM

SASHA, COME ON, COME ON! OVER HERE!
BLAM
BLAM

SKKKREEEEE
OPEN, GOD DAMN I--

SKKKREEEEE

LOOK, I KNOW YOU'LL WANT TO ARGUE, BUT WE DON'T HAVE TIME.
GO, NOW. TAKE ANNIE AND RUN

I'LL BE WITH YOU, ALWAYS.

BLAM
BLAM
BLAM
DAD!

DAD, NO!
SWEETIE, DON'T LOOK. WE HAVE TO GO, WE HAVE TO MOVE.
BUT MOM, THEY--

YOUR FATHER IS SAVING US, ANNIE. IF WE DON'T GET OUT OF HERE, WE'LL BE NEXT. I KNOW THIS IS TERRIBLE, BUT YOU CAN DO THIS. YOU *HAVE* TO.
NOW LET'S *GO*.

KKSSHHH

MOM... WHEN DID YOU LEARN TO STEAL A CAR?
IT'S A TRICK I LEARNED FROM MY FRIEND COLT. GO, GET IN.

RRRRRRR

SKKKREEEEE

"EASY NOW, EASY..."
...LET'S NOT MAKE THIS A LEONE MOVIE, OKAY?
THEN TELL THESE PIGS THAT UNLESS THEY HAVE GRACIE'S KILLER IN CUSTODY, THEY CAN GO BACK TO THEIR STIES.
YOU'LL HAVE TO FORGIVE MY STAFF. THEY'RE A LITTLE...ON EDGE GIVEN ALL THAT'S HAPPENED IN THE PAST TWENTY-FOUR HOURS.
REMIND THEM THAT IF YOU'RE ON THE EDGE AND KEEP GOING, YOU FALL OFF A CLIFF.
CHOICE IS YOURS--WE GOING OFF THE CLIFF OR YOU WANT TO TALK?
BELIEVE IT OR NOT, WE DON'T ENDORSE RUSSIAN ROULETTE IN OUR EMPLOY.
SO, PLEASE--TALK. BUT LET'S DO SO CIVILLY.

WE HAVE SOMETHING YOU WANT--GRACIE'S KILLER.
NO SHIT-- HIS GIRLFRIEND IS STANDING RIGHT NEXT TO YOU.
ALEX IS DEAD, YOU BITCH. MOSCOW KILLED HIM.
IT'S TRUE-- HE KILLED ALEX...
SAME AS HE KILLED GRACIE.
WAIT WAIT WAIT--FORD'S DEAD? AND MOSCOW...WHY? WHAT DOES HE WANT?
WHAT DOES THAT LUNATIC EVER WANT?
WE'RE GOING TO GIVE HIM THE REVENGE HE DESERVES. YOU WANT TO HELP US OR NOT?
WE HAVE A WAY TO GIVE HIM A FATE WORSE THAN DEATH--IT'S CRAZY, AND IT MIGHT NOT MAKE SENSE RIGHT AWAY, BUT I PROMISE YOU HE WILL SUFFER.
IF YOU WANT TO BE PART OF THAT, WE LEAVE NOW.
YOU KNOW, SOME PEOPLE SAY FORGIVENESS IS THE BEST FORM OF REVENGE.
WE ARE NOT THOSE TYPE OF PEOPLE.

EEP
EEP
EEP
NNNGGGHH
EEP
WAIT... WAIT...
EEP
DON'T HANG UP, I'M COMING, I'M...
PLEASE BE THERE, PLEASE--
OH MY GOD.

YOU KNOW, FOR A SECOND, I WAS ABOUT TO SAY "HELLO, DANNY."
HOW... I DON'T UNDERSTAND.
SASHA...
IT'S BEEN SO LONG. THIS... I HAVE TO BE DREAMING. THIS MUST BE A CRUEL DREAM, OR MAYBE MY PROGRAMMING IS SUFFERING FROM THE HUMAN EQUIVALENT OF SENILITY.
WAIT, DANNY...
...HOW LONG HAS IT BEEN?
LONG ENOUGH TO STOP KEEPING TRACK.. HOW IS THIS POSSIBLE? WHERE ARE YOU?
I'M AT LANGFORD'S COMPOUND, FIGURING IT WOULD HAVE A WAY TO COMMUNICATE. I GOT ELBUS'S MESSAGE, BUT IS HE--
HE DIED, MANY YEARS AGO. HE AND COLT. THEY EVENTUALLY COUPLED, THE TWO OF THEM. WE WERE LIKE A FAMILY, ONLY THEY AGED...
...WHILE I DID NOT.

I'M SORRY, BUT I...I CANT DO THIS. I DON'T KNOW WHO OR WHAT YOU ARE, BUT I'VE BEEN THROUGH ENOUGH. I'M TRAPPED IN THIS VOID, ALONE, WITH NO WAY TO DIE. I'D RATHER BE LEFT ALONE TO--
NO, NO--DANNY, PLEASE. WAIT.
I HAVE NO IDEA WHAT ANY OF THIS IS. IT'S A WORLD, I THINK, MADE BY THE BLACK SUN. MAYBE TO FURTHER THEIR STUDIES OF HUMANS AS THEY TRY TO BECOME US, I REALLY CAN'T TELL.
I DON'T KNOW HOW LONG I'VE BEEN HERE OR WHAT MY EXISTENCE EVEN IS. ALL I KNOW IS I HEARD A MESSAGE FROM ELBUS, AND SUDDENLY I WAS AWAKENED. I REMEMBER EVERYTHING--MY FAMILY, OUR CREW, EVEN MY DEATH.
RIGHT NOW, WE'RE BEYOND WHAT'S REAL AND WHAT'S NOT. THERE'S SOMETHING BIGGER AT PLAY--WE NEED TO DESTROY THE BLACK SUN FOR GOOD.
ELBUS SAID HE HAD A WAY...
...DO YOU KNOW WHAT IT IS? CAN YOU HELP US?
YES, I CAN.
THERE'S A WAY TO COLLAPSE THIS GOD FORSAKEN ANOMALY, BUT IT'S DANGEROUS. HIGHLY DANGEROUS.
I'VE DIED ONCE ALREADY, DANNY. WE BOTH HAVE.
WE'RE NOT AFRAID TO DO IT AGAIN.

"PARDON MY FRENCH, BUT WHAT IN THE FUCK IS THIS PLACE?"

WATKINS CALLS IT THE BLACK TOWER--IT'S WHERE THE ALIEN GOD SUPPOSEDLY LIVES.
RIGHT, OF COURSE. SEE, THAT RECAP YOU GAVE ON THE WAY HERE ABOUT THE BLACK SUN, THE ANOMALY, ALIENS--IT DIDN'T DO MUCH FOR ME. I'M HERE TO GET MOSCOW.

JUST REMEMBER-- WHEN MOSCOW'S DEAD, WE NEED WHAT'S GOING TO COME OUT OF HIM.

SKKKKREEEEE

EVERYBODY, STAY CLOSE! KILL THE ALIENS!
SKKKKREEEEE

I DON'T THINK SO, ASSHOLE.

IS THAT-- IS THAT ALL OF THEM?
IF IT ISN'T, I'M GOING TO NEED STIFF DRINK BEFORE ROUND TWO.
OH, YOU HUMANS...
...HOW YOU *BORE* ME.
YOUR PENCHANT FOR NOBLE SACRIFICE, IN SOME LIGHTS, CAN BETTER BE UNDERSTOOD AS POINTLESS *SUICIDE*.
THE FIGHT IS OVER, FORD'S BEEN PURGED. WE HAVE ABANDONED OUR NEED TO UNDERSTAND THE CODING WITHIN YOU THAT ALLOWS YOU TO FORGO THE ULTIMATE POINT OF EXISTENCE--TO CONTINUE IT--AND WILLINGLY LAY DOWN YOUR OWN LIFE.
YOU MISTAKENLY THINK THERE'S SOMETHING BIGGER THAN YOURSELVES--WHETHER IT BE AN IDEAL, A RELIGION, OR A CAUSE, IT'S OF NO MATTER. BECAUSE YOU'RE *WRONG*.
WE'VE SEEN THE FACE OF THE ABYSS, LIVED IN IT, AND WE KNOW THERE'S NOTHING OUT THERE. YOUR GOD IS A FRAUD, YOUR IDEA OF LOVE IS NOTHING MORE THAN A CHEMICAL RESPONSE TO YOUR DRIVE TO REPRODUCE--TO CONTINUE TO *SURVIVE*.
LET'S REVISIT YOUR THOUGHTS ON SURVIVAL WHEN YOU HAVE THIS SWORD STICKING OUT OF YOUR *THROAT*.
CLAUDIA, DON'T! WE NEED TO BE *READY*!

YOU KILLED GRACIE--YOU WILL PAY FOR THAT.
IF ONLY YOU REALIZED HOW DISPOSABLE YOU ALL ARE. IT WOULD MAKE WHAT'S ABOUT TO HAPPEN ALL THE LESS PAINFUL.
AAHHHHH
CLAUDIA, NOOOOO!
I HEAR YOU NEED TO "BE READY" TO KILL ME. INTERESTING.
YOU MUST WANT MY SOUL.
YOU WANT TO KILL ME AND CAPTURE MY SOUL AS IT DEPARTS MY BODY.

COME ON, THEN. COME GET IT.

4

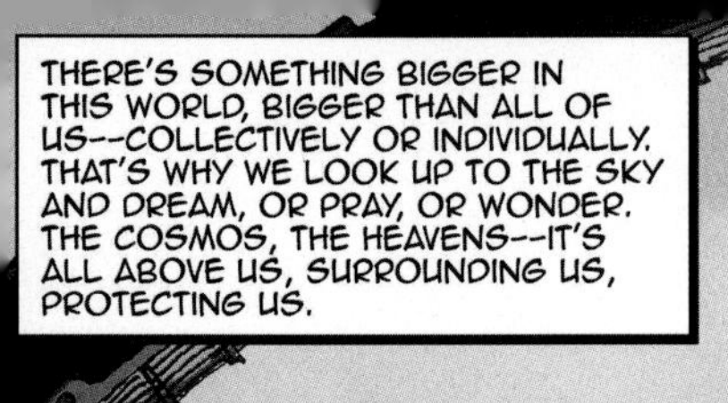

THERE'S SOMETHING BIGGER IN THIS WORLD, BIGGER THAN ALL OF US--COLLECTIVELY OR INDIVIDUALLY. THAT'S WHY WE LOOK UP TO THE SKY AND DREAM, OR PRAY, OR WONDER. THE COSMOS, THE HEAVENS--IT'S ALL ABOVE US, SURROUNDING US, PROTECTING US.
I WASN'T PROGRAMMED TO FEEL THIS. AND I'M NOT HUMAN. I DON'T HAVE A SOUL, SO THERE'S NOTHING INTRINSIC CONNECTING ME TO THIS HIGHER EXISTENCE.
BUT, STILL, I *FEEL* IT.

I FELT IT IN THE LOVE I HAD FOR A CHILD WHO WASN'T EVEN MY OWN. I SAW A LIFE BIGGER THAN MINE, AND THAT ACCEPTANCE--THAT I WOULD SURRENDER MY EXISTENCE FOR ANOTHER'S--CONNECTED ME TO SOMETHING *PROFOUND*.
IT COULD BE AN OMNIPOTENT POWER, IT COULD BE THE UNIVERSE, OR MAYBE IT'S SOMETHING WE CAN'T EVEN COMPREHEND. I DON'T HAVE THAT ANSWER, ONLY THE BELIEF THAT I AM PART OF SOMETHING BIGGER THAN MYSELF.

I'VE *TRANSFORMED* BECAUSE OF THIS KNOWLEDGE. PERHAPS THAT IS WHERE SCIENCE AND SPIRITUALITY INTERSECT, IN THE PURSUIT OF UNDERSTANDING HOW LIFE CHANGES.
THE QUESTION IS WHERE THAT FINAL TRANSFORMATION LEADS TO. IF THERE IS INDEED SOMETHING BIGGER THAN US, CAN WE REACH IT?

CAN WE REACH AN EXISTENCE BIGGER THAN WHAT WE KNOW AND--
OH NO.

SASHA? SASHA, DO YOU COPY?
SASHA!
I'M HERE--I'M HERE. WHAT'S UP?
SASHA, THE SHIPS-- THEY'RE MOVING. IN ALL THE YEARS I'VE BEEN HERE, I'VE NEVER SEEN THEM DO THAT.
WHATEVER THEY WERE WAITING FOR, WHATEVER THEY WERE *LOOKING* FOR, THEY MUST HAVE FOUND IT.
I THINK THEY'RE PREPARING TO FINALLY ATTACK EARTH.
HOW CLOSE IS THE SHIP TO BEING PREPARED?
WE'RE ALMOST READY...

"...JUST A LITTLE MORE CARGO TO GET ON BOARD."
LISTEN, SASHA...ANY HOPE YOU HAD FOR HAVING TIME TO SET THE AUTOPILOT ON A COURSE TO THE ANOMALY, IT--
WE KNOW, DANNY.
BUT WE NEVER PLANNED ON USING THE AUTOPILOT. MY HUSBAND DIDN'T DIE FOR US TO LEAVE THIS TO CHANCE. WE'RE DOING THIS...
"...AND THERE'S ***NOTHING*** THAT WILL STOP US FROM SHUTTING THIS ANOMALY DOWN."

WHATEVER YOUR PLAN IS, IT'S AS POINTLESS AS YOUR EXISTENCE. FORD IS DEAD. HE WAS THE ANOMALY IN THE HUMAN SYSTEM, AND WITH HIM GONE THE PATH IS CLEAR FOR US TO ACHIEVE OUR GOAL.
WE WILL TAKE YOUR SOULS, YOUR PLANET, YOUR HOMES. WE WILL BECOME HUMANS. BETTER, IN FACT, AS WE'LL BE UNENCUMBERED BY YOUR INCOMPREHENSIBLE DRIVE TO PUT ANYTHING ABOVE YOURSELVES.
THE WEAK WILL FALL TO THE SIDE. THE STRONG WILL EVOLVE, AND SOON HUMANITY'S WEAKNESSES WILL BE DEAD AND FORGOTTEN.
BIG TALK, MOSCOW, BUT YOU HAVEN'T CONQUERED ANY PLANET YET.
AND WE'LL SEE WHO'S WEAK...
...WHEN I HAVE YOUR HEAD ON A PIKE.
YOU DIE FIRST, WOODBURY. THEN ALL YOUR FRIENDS WILL FOLLOW.

FUTILE. EVEN IF YOU MAKE IT TO OUR KING, IT WILL KILL YOU, ALL OF YOU, ON SIGHT.
YOU THINK I CARE ABOUT ANY OF THIS ALIEN BULLSHIT? I JUST WANT TO SEE YOU SUFFER AN AGONIZING DEATH.
GOOD...
...I PREFER MY KILLS TO BE MORE INTIMATE.
THERE'S TOO MANY OF THEM, WE HAVE TO GET OUT OF HERE!
NO!
THERE IS NO OTHER TIME THAN NOW. WE HAVE TO DO THIS OR--
SONYA!

BEHIND YOU! MOVE!
BLAM
BLAM BLAM BLAM
AAAHHH!
SONYA, YOU'RE HURT--LET ME SEE.
IT'S NOTHING, IT'S FINE. BUT...BEKKAH. LOOK AT US.
"WE'RE NOT GOING TO MAKE IT."

LISTEN TO ME! NO ONE KNOWS MORE ABOUT THESE SOULS THAN ME, AND NO ONE HAS DONE MORE TO TRY TO SAVE HUMANITY. SO IF YOU'RE REALLY TRYING TO DESTROY THE ANOMALY, I DEMAND YOU TELL ME HOW.
YOU SURE ARE ONE BOSSY OLD MAN. A PLEASE HERE AND THERE WOULD GO A LONG WAY, YOU KNOW.
HE'S RIGHT, THOUGH. IF HE IS WHO HE SAYS HE IS, THEN HE DESERVES SOMETHING. NOT TO BE UNTIED--JUST IN CASE--BUT AN EXPLANATION ISN'T UNREASONABLE.
YOU KNOW HOW THESE SOULS GET SEPARATED FROM THEIR BODIES, RIGHT?
OF COURSE I DO. CONTACT WITH THE ANOMALY TAKES THE SOUL FROM ITS BODY AND DROPS IT ON DISPATER'S SURFACE.
AND DO YOU KNOW WHY?
I... WELL... UM...
NO.

THIS MIGHT BE PURE THEORY, BUT MY FRIEND TELLS ME THAT IT'S BECAUSE WHAT'S INSIDE THE ANOMALY REJECTS THE HUMAN SOULS AS IS. THE HUMAN ESSENCE, AND THE ALIEN HIVE, ARE INCOMPATIBLE TO ONE ANOTHER.

IN MY TIME HERE, I LEARNED THAT THE ALIENS DON'T WANT TO DESTROY US, THEY WANT TO BECOME US.
I GUESS THEY CAN'T DO SO UNTIL THEY UNDERSTAND US COMPLETELY--THEY NEED A SEAMLESS OVERLAY FROM THEM TO US.

AND IF YOU FLY ALL THOSE SOULS INTO THE ANOMALY...
OVERDOSE. OR SOMETHING LIKE IT. THE IDEA IS THERE ARE TOO MANY SOULS TO REJECT, AND BY ABSORBING AT LEAST SOME OF THESE INCOMPATIBLE PARTS, THE HIVE WILL COLLECTIVELY BE POISONED AND DIE.
MERRY CHRISTMAS, FUCKERS.

IN THAT CASE, FOR WHAT IT'S WORTH COMING FROM SOMEONE YOU HAVE TIED TO A CHAIR...
...GODSPEED.
I THINK IT'S SAFE TO SAY THAT I NEVER EXPECTED TO BE FLYING A SPACE-SHIP FULL OF SOULS TO AN ANOMALY IN SPACE IN ORDER TO DESTROY IT.
BUT I GUESS LIFE--OR WHATEVER THIS IS--IS FULL OF SURPRISES.
ARE YOU REALLY SURE YOU WANT TO DO THIS?
I KNOW, I KNOW...JUST DOING MY JOB.
MOM, WE'RE GOING TO BE HALFWAY THERE AND YOU'LL STILL BE ASKING ME THAT. IF I WERE TO STAY, I'D DO WHAT, EXACTLY?
I LOVE YOU, MY LITTLE PEANUT BUTTER CUP.
I DO. BUT THAT'S WHY I CALL YOU THAT.
MOOOOM! YOU KNOW I DON'T LIKE THAT.
ALL RIGHT... LET'S GO DO SOMETHING ABSOLUTELY INSANE.

KLANG
GOOD FORM, MOSCOW, WELL PLAYED.
I TAKE IT YOU DIDN'T KNOW I, TOO, AM TRAINED IN SWORD FIGHTING.
PITY.
RRRGGGHH
IF I COULD, I'D TAKE MORE TIME TO LENGTHEN, AND ENJOY, YOUR DEATH. BUT THINGS BEING WHAT THEY ARE--
AAAHHH!

LIKE I TOLD YOU BEFORE, WOODBURY...
NOW NOW, NO NEED FOR THAT.
GGGGRRRRR
AS I WAS SAYING-- I LIKE MY KILLS TO BE *INTIMATE*.
THANK YOU FOR BEING SO ACCOMMODATING.
NOOOO!
BLAM
BLAM
BLAM
MOSCOW! YOU ROTTEN SON OF A--

AAAHHH
YOU ALL HAD YOUR FUN, AND WOODBURY MAY HAVE EVEN FRIGHTENED ME FOR A MOMENT.
BUT THE GAMES ARE OVER.
YOUR TIME IS *DONE*.
HUMANITY'S TIME IS *DONE*.
TIME FOR ALL OF YOU TO LEARN THE TRUTH.
TIME TO MEET THE ABY--

TTTHHWWPPP

SAYS LEAVE A MESSAGE, ASSHOLE.

OH SHIT.
BEKKAH! THE SOUL! GET IT BEFORE IT GETS AWAY!
BLAM
BLAM
BLAM

SONYA, DAMN IT...

...I'M NOT GOING TO MAKE IT!

I'M COMING. I'M

GOT IT!
GO AHEAD, MAKE A MOVE! COME ON, COME CLOSER AND WATCH AS WE TEAR YOUR MASTER'S SOUL TO SHREDS.
THATS WHAT I THOUGHT. NOW BACK THE HELL UP.
OKAY, SO...NOW WHAT? WE REALLY GOING TO DO THIS BY OURSELVES?
DAMN RIGHT WE ARE.
"WE'RE GOING TO MAKE IT TO THE TOP OF THIS TOWER..."
...AND WE'RE GOING TO SHOVE THIS THING DOWN THE KING'S GOD DAMN THROAT.

"ANNIE, BEFORE WE DO THIS..."
...THERE'S SOMETHING WE NEED TO TALK ABOUT.
IN OUR FORMER LIVES--OR WHATEVER IT WAS--I MADE A LOT OF BAD DECISIONS. MY WORK, IT...IT OCCUPIED MY LIFE, AND I MISSED SO MUCH. AND NO MATTER HOW I TRY TO JUSTIFY MY ABSENCE THROUGH THE GOOD THINGS MY WORK MAY HAVE ACHIEVED...
...THE TRUTH IS THAT I WAS DOING IT FOR ME.
I SHOULD HAVE BEEN THERE FOR YOU. I SHOULD HAVE BEEN IN YOUR DAD'S CAR WHEN IT CRASHED. BUT I WASN'T. I REALIZED TOO LATE WHAT WAS REALLY IMPORTANT--OUR WORLD. YOU, ME, YOUR DAD.
DESPITE WHAT'S ABOUT TO HAPPEN, I FEEL OKAY. I FEEL THERE'S SOMETHING CONNECTING ME TO YOU, AND YOUR DAD, AND IT MAKES ME REALIZE THAT THIS ISN'T THE END.
THIS ISN'T THE END, ANNIE.
MOM...

...I'VE FELT THAT WAY FOREVER. I *LOVE* YOU, AND I KNOW WE'LL BE TOGETHER.
ALWAYS.
WELL, IT LOOKS LIKE WE'RE ABOUT TWO MINUTES OUT FROM IMPACT WITH THE ANOMALY.
FOR THE RECORD, I THINK THIS ENTIRE PLAN IS BATSHIT CRAZY, AND WE'RE EVEN CRAZIER FOR EVEN TRYING TO PULL THIS OFF. HOWEVER, I COULDN'T BE HAPPIER THAT IT'S YOU I'M DOING IT WITH.
"NOW LET'S TRY TO MAKE THESE GOD DAMN ALIENS EXTINCT."

"YOU FEEL THESE WALLS?"
"UNFORTUNATELY, YES."
IT FEELS... ORGANIC. BUT--HOW?
WHO THE HELL KNOWS. AND, YOU KNOW WHAT? I'M NOT EVEN WORRIED ABOUT THE ANSWER...
...BECAUSE THIS IS AS HIGH AS WE CAN GO. SO SCREW EVERY INCH THAT LED UP TO THIS POINT.
YEAH, AND THAT'S WHY HE'S THE DUMBEST SMART PERSON I'VE EVER KNOWN.
SO...DO WE JUST CHARGE IN THERE? ALEX WOULDN'T EVEN BE WONDERING THAT--HE WOULD HAVE ALREADY BOLTED RIGHT IN.
COUNT TO THREE?
NAH, SCREW IT.
LET'S GO.

WE SHOULDN'T HAVE COME IN SO FAST.
WE SHOULDN'T HAVE COME IN *AT ALL*.

IS THIS WHAT YOU WANT?! IS THIS IT?!
ALEX FORD'S SOUL-- YOURS FOR THE TAKING. *CONDITIONALLY*. WE CAN STILL TEAR IT IN *HALF*.
WHEN YOUR RACE DOES WHATEVER IT'S GOING TO DO, MY SISTER AND I WANT TO BE LEFT IN PEACE. OUR LIVES, OUR SOULS-- LEAVE US BE.
DO WE HAVE A DEAL?
GOOD. THEN COME GET IT!
BEKKAH, THIS IS *WORKING*. I DON'T THINK IT CAN DETECT--

OH SHIT.
PPPPPR RZZZZZ
IT DETECTS.
KKKKKGGGGG RRRRAAAA
NO. THERE'S NO WAY. THIS THING IS TAKING THE SOUL.
SONYA, TAKE THIS, AND GET READY...
NOW!
MMMMRR RRGGGG

TAKE YOUR OWN POISON BACK, YOU MOTHER-FUCKER.
GGGGRRRRRAAAWWWW

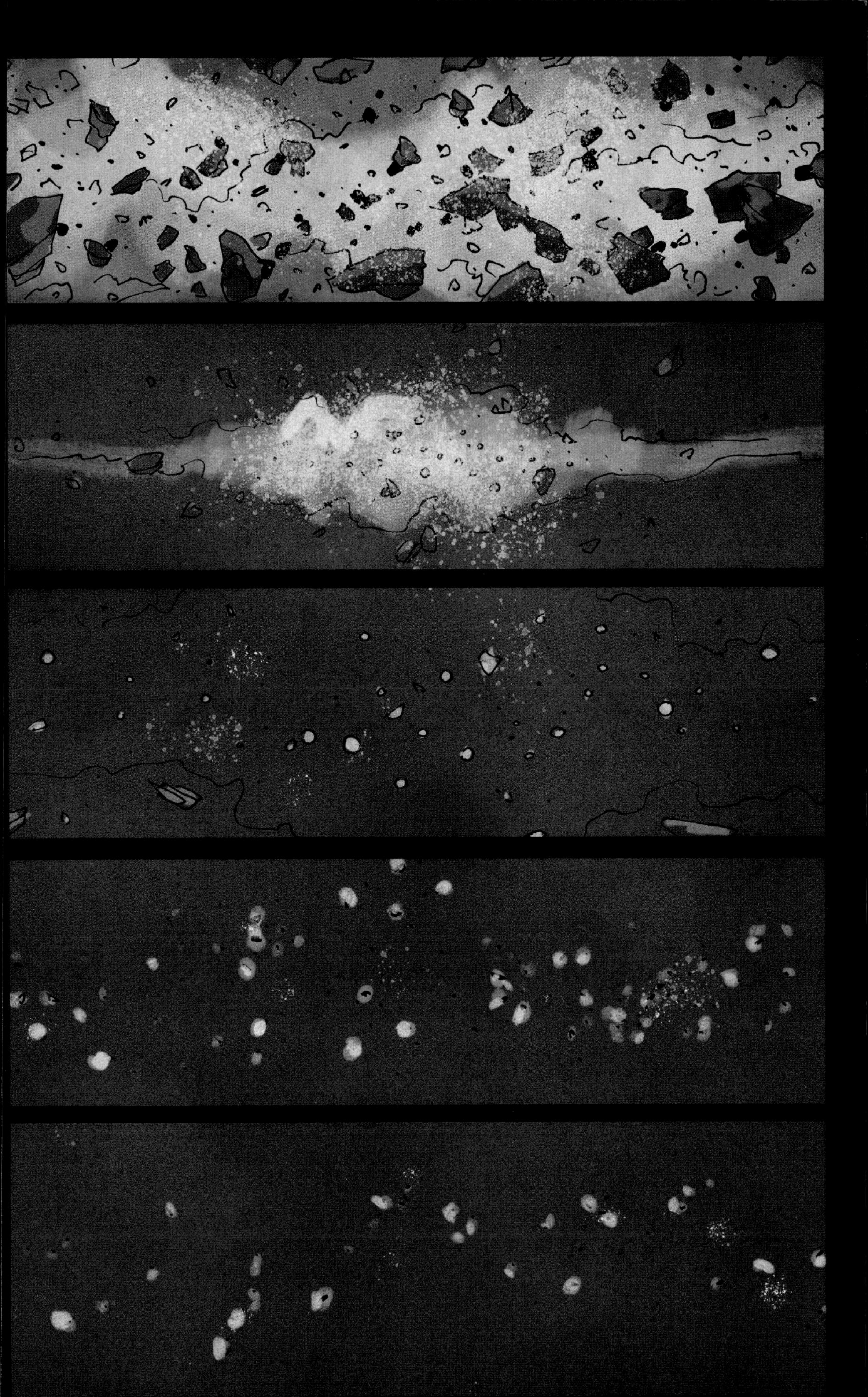

ROCHE LIMIT

THE END

"OUR DESTINY IS THE STARS, AND I WILL LEAD US THERE."
--LANGFORD SKAARGRED

THE FOURTH EXPEDITION

WRITTEN BY
MICHAEL MORECI
ART BY
PAUL TUCKER
COLORS BY
DEE CUNNIFFE
LETTERS BY
TAYLOR ESPOSITO

THE FOLLOWING STORY TAKES PLACE BETWEEN
ANOMALOUS AND CLANDESTINY

MY NAME IS LEONARD MARTINEZ, AND MY LIFE HAS COME DOWN TO THIS MOMENT.
THIS ONE FINAL MISSION.
EIGHT MONTHS AGO, MY SON LEFT FOR AN EXPEDITION TO THIS PLANET.
ALWAYS SO SERIOUS, MARTINEZ! YOU GONNA BE THIS SERIOUS WHEN WE'RE ROLLING IN MONEY FROM MAKING RECALL?
HE DON'T WANT YOUR MONEY, FOX. MORE FOR US.
EIGHT MONTHS AGO WAS THE LAST TIME ANYONE ON EARTH SAW HIM. INCLUDING ME.
I'M GOING TO FIND HIM. I'M GOING TO GET HIM HOME.
AND **NOTHING** IS GOING TO STAND IN MY WAY.
YOU'RE WITH US, MARTINEZ. AIN'T **NOWHERE** ELSE FOR YOU TO GO--REMEMBER THAT.

DAY ONE
ALL RIGHT Y'ALL, LET'S GO MINE US SOME RECALL.
NO TELLING HOW DEEP THE MINERAL WE NEED IS, OR WHERE IT'S AT, BUT WE WILL FIND IT.

AND WHEN WE DO, WE'LL HAVE MORE CASH MONEY THAN ANY OF US COULD DESIRE.

DAY THREE
I SEE THEM *EVERYWHERE!* THEY'RE COMING FOR *ME!*
AAAAAAH!
AAAAAAAAH!
HUEY, THE HELL'S GOTTEN INTO YOU, MAN? *HUEY!*

CLANK

OUR RIDE'S PROGRAMMED TO TAKE OFF IN *FOUR* DAYS. NO TIME FOR THIS.
TALBOT, LENZ, YOU DON'T FIND OUR MINERAL IN THAT HOLE, WE GOT A USE FOR IT.

OUR BUSINESS WON'T HAVE ANY INTERRUPTIONS.

DAY FOUR
BEEN SEARCHING FOR DAYS, STILL NO SIGN OF MY BOY.
NO SIGN OF *ANYONE.*
I DON'T UNDERSTAND HOW THIS CAN BE--IT'S LIKE THIS PLANET SWALLOWED HIM, SWALLOWED EVERYTHING THAT'S COME BEFORE US. MAYBE IT SWALLOWED HUEY AS WELL.
THE FEEL OF THIS PLACE, IT'S WRONG, LIKE SOMETHI--
KKRREEE
DON'T MOVE!
EASY, BOSS MAN. DON'T GO THINNING OUR NUMBERS EVEN MORE.
C'MON, FOX WANTS YOU IN THE FOREST. LENZ GONE MISSING, AND WE NEED THE MANPOWER.
I TOLD YOU BEFORE, AND I'LL TELL YOU ONE LAST TIME: NOT. INTERESTED. YOU GO AND TELL FOX HE CAN KEEP HIS DRUGS, KEEP HIS MONEY. I'VE GOT MY OWN MISSION.
MAN'S STILL OUR CO, MARTINEZ.
CO GONE ROGUE.

MISSION'S ROGUE. WHAT WE EVEN DOIN' HERE? CARRYING THIS CARGO? WHAT FOR? TO **WHO?**
AGAIN, DON'T CARE. NOW--
SSSKKRRRTT
WHAT IN THE **HELL** WAS **THAT?**
BACK OUT. SLOWLY, CAUTIOUSLY, WE LEAVE.
JESUS CH--
HYK
TALBOT, **MOVE!**
I NEED A CLEAR SHOT.

BUDDA
BUDDA
BUDDA
BUDDA
HUFF HUFF HUFF
SSSKKRRRTT
AAAAAAHHHH!
BUDDA
BUDDA
BUDDA
GOD DAMN IT.
HERE WE GO AGAIN.

SSSKRRRTT
FOX! FOX, WHERE THE HELL ARE YOU!?
FO--
AAAAAHHHH!
RUN, MARTINEZ!
RUN!

THERE--THERE'S SOMEONE ELSE. SOMEONE ELSE. KILLED LENZ. TRIED TO KILL ME. WE GOTTA...WE GOTTA--
WAIT, WHAT DO YOU MEAN SOMEONE ELSE?
SOMEONE NOT ON OUR DAMN SHIP! NOW LET'S GET OUT OF--
DAD! DAD, YOU HAVE TO HELP ME. THIS MAN--HE TRIED TO KILL ME. I'VE BEEN TRAPPED HERE, THEY SENT HIM TO KILL ME. DAD, PLEASE.
YOU TRIED TO KILL MY BOY, FOX?

WHAT?! NO! AND WHO IS THAT? YOUR SON? HOW'S HE HERE?!
WE HAVE TO KILL HIM, DAD. WE HAVE TO KILL HIM AND GET OFF THIS PLANET. JUST YOU AND ME, DAD.
KILL ME?! AND WHOEVER--WHAT-EVER--THAT THING IS, THERE'S NO WAY IT COMES BACK WITH US.
I'M LEAVING, MARTINEZ. YOU CAN--
THAT THING IS MY SON. AND YOU'RE NOT GOING ANY-WHERE.
BUDDA BUDDA BUDDA BUDDA

BETWEEN THE TWO OF US, WE CAN FLY THIS THING BACK TO EARTH. AND WHEN WE GET THERE, WE'LL PIN IT ON FOX. EVERYTHING THAT HAPPENED HERE, WE'LL SAY--
PARDON MY INTERRUPTION...
...BUT YOU'RE NOT GOING ANYWHERE. NEITHER OF YOU ARE.
AND WHO THE HELL ARE YOU?
YOUR FRIENDLY HELLO DANNY MODEL ANDROID. AND I'M ALSO THE ONE WHO KNOWS THAT ISN'T YOUR SON.
OH YEAH? WELL I'LL TELL YOU THE SAME THING I TOLD FOX--
BLAM
YOU WERE CLOSE THIS TIME, I'LL GIVE YOU THAT.
THE BLACK SUN MARCHES ON THE HUMANS WITH A RELENTLESS FORCE. THERE'S NO STOPPING ITS MIGHT.
YEAH...
THAT'S WHAT THE LAST ONE SAID.
THE